STARTING OVER IN SUNSET PARK

Story by José Pelaez and Lynn McGee • Pictures by Bianca Diaz

TILBURY HOUSE PUBLISHERS, THOMASTON, MAINE

Text © 2021 by José Pelaez and Lynn McGee • Illustrations © 2021 by Bianca Diaz

Hardcover ISBN 978-0-88448-844-6

Tilbury House Publishers • www.tilburyhouse.com

Library of Congress Control Number: 2020951281

Designed by Frame25 Productions
Printed in China

10 9 8 7 6 5 4 3 2 1

My first trip in an airplane was from the Dominican Republic to New York City. It was just me and my mom, and we were on our way to Sunset Park, Brooklyn, where my aunts and uncles and cousins live.

When we arrived, I could see that their lives in this new place were beautiful.

Could my life here be beautiful as well? I didn't know.
I only knew that I was homesick and a little afraid.

Mama and I were invited to stay with my aunt and cousins until we found an apartment of our own.

We were thankful, but we felt like we were in the way.

"Mama," I kept saying, "*Echo de menos muestra casa.*" (I miss our home.)

"When I get a job," Mama answered, "we'll have our own place.

Be patient, *mi corazoncito.*" (Be patient, my heart.)

My aunt told Mama about a factory in Brooklyn that makes decorations for all the holidays in America. Even though it was summer, they were making Christmas decorations. My mom has a lot of talent, so of course she was hired!

While she worked, I waited for her in my aunt's apartment, missing home.

When Mama got her first paycheck, we began to look for our own apartment.
A realtor showed us places that Mama said were in our price range.

Still, I missed the DR, and I missed *mi abuela* (my grandmother) and her house—the cats, the mangos, the papayas, the wild parrots, and her delicious meals: the *mangú* (plantain mash) and *habichuelas con dulce* (sweet cream of beans).

"Cuando estés triste, agita esta maraca y recuerda que habrá muchos buenos momentos en tu futuro," Grandma told me before we left. (When you are sad, shake this maraca and remember that there will be many good times in your future.)

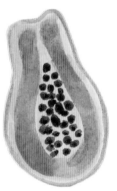

She tried to hide it from me, but I knew that Mama was homesick too.

When school began, I started learning English, but not fast enough.
Everyone was ahead of me, and sometimes I couldn't understand the teacher.

I missed my friends and my old neighborhood in the DR more and more. Even the trees here were different, and nobody knew what a good soccer player I was.

One day in class, the teacher asked me for something, but I didn't know what she wanted. A classmate whispered, "*¡La profesora le está pidiendo sus deberes de matemáticas!*" (The teacher is asking for your math homework!)

Everyone looked at me. My throat got tight and tears started to well up. It was so quiet while the teacher waited for me to speak. I felt mad and scared, and I cried, "*¡Bruja!*" (Witch!)

"*Hablemos,*" the teacher said in a kinder voice. "*Tú, yo y tu madre.*" (Let's talk—you, me, and your mother.)

I knew I was in trouble, but hearing the teacher speak Spanish made me feel a little better.

"*Créame, yo pasé por lo mismo*," the teacher said when Mama came to school. (Believe me, I went through the same thing.)

"Thank you," said Mama, "but I speak English." Then she turned to me and said, "Tell Mrs. Kowalski you're sorry for calling her a witch."

"*Lamento haberle llamado bruja*," I said.

"*¡En inglés!*" Mama murmured.

"I'm sorry, Mrs. Kowalski."

"I understand," Mrs. Kowalski said. "I went through the same thing when I moved to New York from Poland as a little girl. You're going to be fine. It will take a few months, but we will work together to help you catch up."

Mama helped me, too. I worked hard, and I practiced my English all the time!
We started to make friends in our new neighborhood.

One day Mama and I met our neighbor Mr. Palmieri, who lived in the apartment above ours. He was carrying a huge puppet head.

"*¿Hizo usted esa máscara?*" I asked him. (Did you make that mask?)

Mr. Palmieri smiled. "Yes, I did—with my own hands! I made them as a boy in Puerto Rico for the Vejigante festivals in my hometown. I have many more at home, and you and your mama are welcome to visit and see them."

Mr. Palmieri told me to call him Javier. Señor Javier's apartment was a magical place, but the giant cat in the corner was the most magical thing of all.

"You have a cat!" I exclaimed.

"He's a tuxedo cat," Javier said, "and he is my house guest. His mom and dad are on vacation, so he's staying with me for a while."

"You are babysitting him?" Mama asked.

Javier nodded happily. "It's a little side gig for me. I feel lonely, and then I have a kitty friend who comes to stay with me and I feel better. Also," he said, glancing at Mama, "the money doesn't hurt."

"People pay you for that?" Mama asked in wonder.

Javier shrugged. "Isn't America wonderful?"

Mama and Javier laughed. Then Mama asked, "If you get too many cat-sitting requests, could we maybe help?"

The next day Señor Javier visited our apartment. "You understand," he said after looking around, "that before I send you a cat, you have to get window screens."

"I will talk to our landlord right away," Mama said.

After that, we always had a kitty staying with us. They were shy at first.

"Give the kitty some space," Mama would say. "Let her adjust."

Every holiday, Mama brought home decorations she had made at work.

This strange new place began to feel a little magical.

The day we went to Central Park, it began to snow. I had never seen snow before. Mama had never seen it either. It felt so cold and soft.

Mama got better at her job and felt more confident.

I felt happier, too.

I still missed Grandma and my beautiful island, but Sunset Park, Brooklyn, started to feel like a good place for me.

Just like the cats, I was getting used to my new home.

Starting over in Sunset Park was
hard, but in the end it was good.

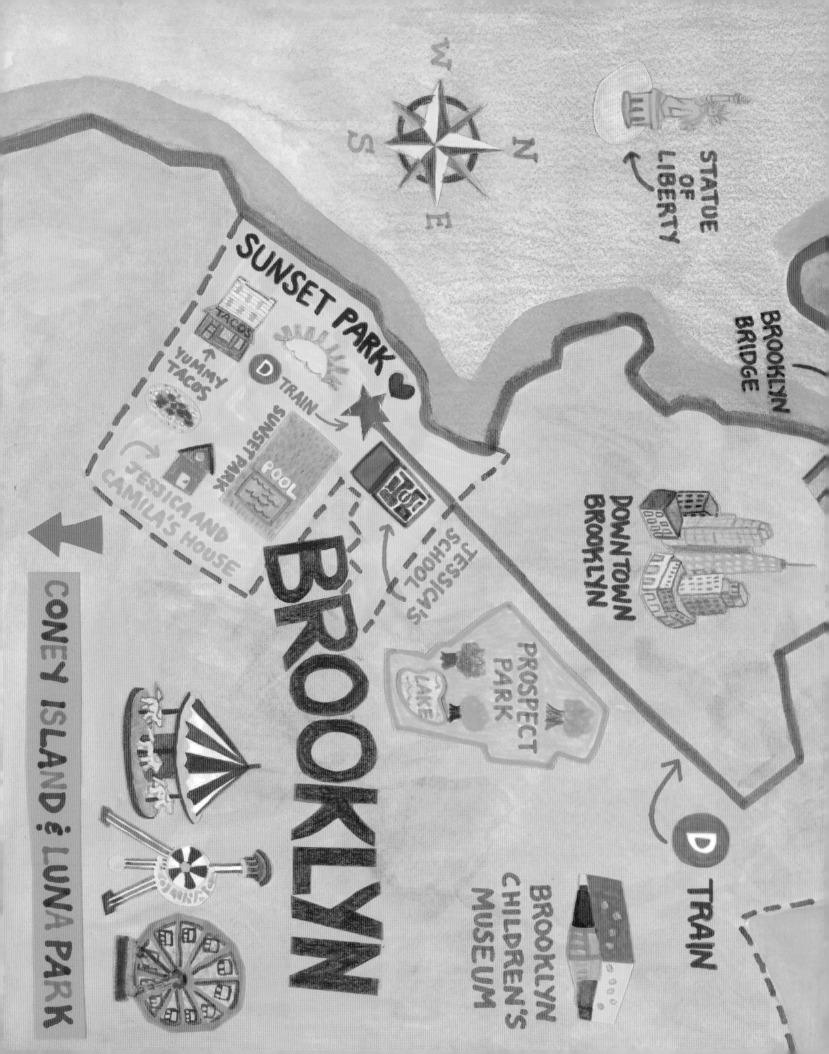

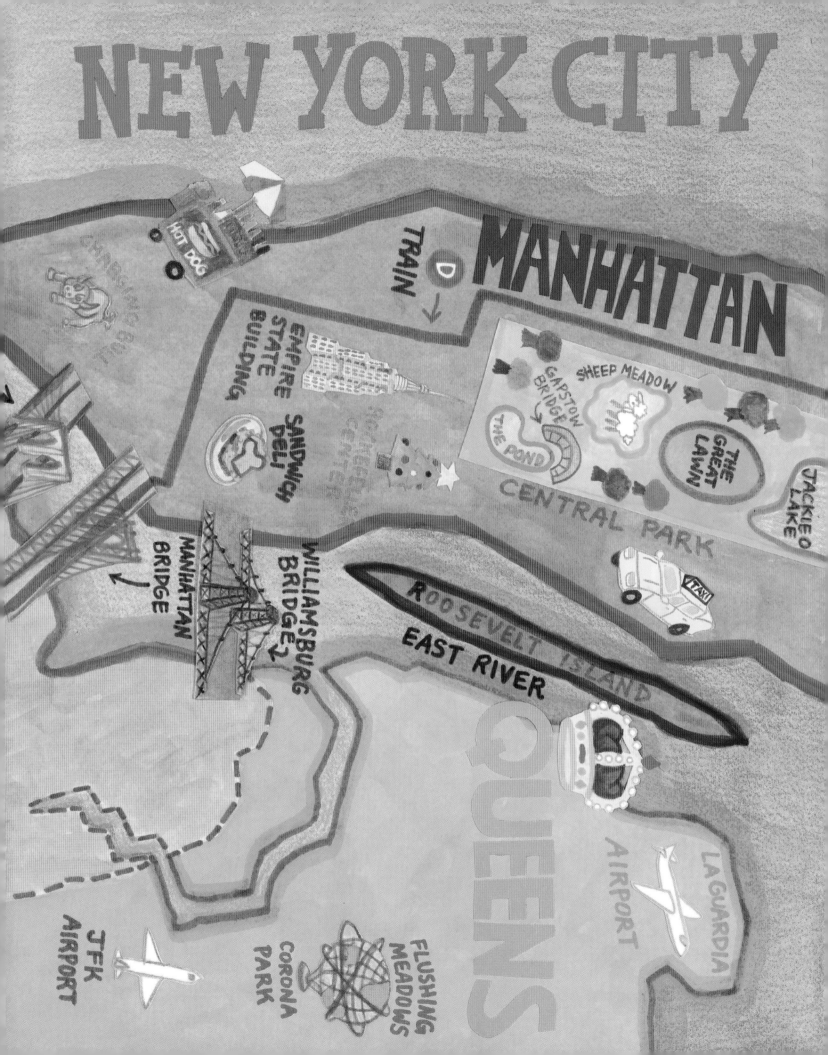

Immigration Resources

The following organizations provide information and help to immigrants and those who want to learn more about immigration:

American Immigration Council
www.americanimmigrationcouncil.org

Amnesty International
www.amnesty.org

Bipartisan Policy Center
https://bipartisanpolicy.org

The Center for Immigration Studies
https://cis.org

Human Rights Watch
www.hrw.org

Immigrant Legal Resource Center
www.ilrc.org

International Rescue Committee
www.rescue.org

National Partnership for New Americans
http://partnershipfornewamericans.org

United We Dream
https://unitedwedream.org

José Pelaez, a native of Madrid, has lived in Paris, London, Torino, and New York City. Dealing with his own cats' needs during those moves inspired him to found Kitty in NY, an agency that provides temporary homes to the pets of traveling New Yorkers. *Starting Over in Sunset Park*, his first children's book, explores issues he himself experienced while adjusting to a new life in America.

Lynn McGee's published volumes of poetry include *Tracks* (2019), *Sober Cooking* (2016), and two award-winning chapbooks. Twice a Pushcart nominee, she has taught adult literacy to immigrants and has led poetry workshops in New York City elementary schools as an artist-in-residence with the Teachers & Writers Collaborative. *Starting Over in Sunset Park* is her first children's book.

Bianca Diaz, a granddaughter of Mexican immigrants, grew up in Pilsen, a Mexican American neighborhood in Chicago, and now lives in Brooklyn. Bianca received the Ezra Jack Keats New Illustrator Honor 2018 award for her first children's book, *The One Day House*.